The Tiara Club

✦ AT SILVER TOWERS ✦

The Tiara Club

Princess Charlotte *and the* Birthday Ball

Princess Katie *and the* Silver Pony

Princess Daisy *and the* Dazzling Dragon

Princess Sophia *and the* Sparkling Surprise

Princess Alice *and the* Magical Mirror

Princess Emily *and the* Substitute Fairy

———❦———

The Tiara Club at Silver Towers

Princess Charlotte *and the* Enchanted Rose

Princess Katie *and the* Mixed-up Potion

Princess Daisy *and the* Magical Merry-Go-Round

Princess Alice *and the* Glass Slipper

Princess Sophia *and the* Prince's Party

VIVIAN FRENCH

The Tiara Club

AT SILVER TOWERS

Princess Emily
AND THE
Wishing Star

ILLUSTRATED BY SARAH GIBB

KATHERINE TEGEN BOOKS
HarperTrophy®
An Imprint of HarperCollins*Publishers*

Harper Trophy® is a registered trademark of
HarperCollins Publishers.

The Tiara Club at Silver Towers:
Princess Emily and the Wishing Star
Text copyright © 2007 by Vivian French
Illustrations copyright © 2007 by Sarah Gibb

Library of Congress Cataloging-in-Publication Data
French, Vivian.
Princess Emily and the Wishing Star / by Vivian French ; illus-
trated by Sarah Gibb. — 1st U.S. ed.
p. cm. — (Tiara Club at Silver Towers)
"Katherine Tegen books."
Summary: Princess Emily and her friends at the Royal
Academy receive their silver sashes after Emily helps horrible
twins, Gruella and Diamonde, make up following a fight.
ISBN 978-0-06-112451-8
[1. Princesses—Fiction. 2. Friendship—Fiction. 3. Rites and
ceremonies—Fiction.] I. Gibb, Sarah, ill. II. Title.
PZ7.F88917Prg 2007   2007011864
[Fic]—dc22   CIP
                                                        AC

Typography by Amy Ryan
❖
First U.S. edition, 2007

*For a truly magical and
very starry Princess Christine, xx
—V.F.*

*For my big sis, Princess Charlotte
—S.G.*

The Royal Palace Academy
for the Preparation of Perfect Princesses
(Known to our students as "The Princess Academy")

OUR SCHOOL MOTTO:
*A Perfect Princess always thinks of others before herself,
and is kind, caring, and truthful.*

Silver Towers offers a complete education for
Tiara Club princesses with emphasis on
selected outings. The curriculum includes:

Fans and Curtseys

*A visit to Witch Windlespin
(Royal herbalist, healer, and maker of magic potions)*

Problem Prime Ministers

*A visit to the Museum of Royal Life
(Students will be well protected from the Poisoned Apple)*

Our principal, Queen Samantha Joy, is present
at all times, and students are in the excellent care
of the school Fairy Godmother, Fairy Angora.

OUR RESIDENT STAFF & VISITING EXPERTS INCLUDE:

LADY ALBINA MacSPLINTER *(School Secretary)*
CROWN PRINCE DANDINO *(Field Trips)*
QUEEN MOTHER MATILDA *(Etiquette, Posture, and Poise)*
FAIRY G. *(Head Fairy Godmother)*

We award tiara points to encourage our
Tiara Club princesses toward the next level.
All princesses who win enough points at Silver
Towers will attend the Silver Ball, where they
will be presented with their Silver Sashes.

Silver Sash Tiara Club princesses are invited
to return to Ruby Mansions, our exclusive
residence for Perfect Princesses, where they may
continue their education at a higher level.

PLEASE NOTE:

Princesses are expected to arrive
at the Academy with a *minimum* of:

TWENTY BALL GOWNS
*(with all necessary hoops,
petticoats, etc.)*

TWELVE DAY-DRESSES

SEVEN GOWNS
*suitable for garden parties
and other special daytime
occasions*

TWELVE TIARAS

DANCING SHOES
five pairs

VELVET SLIPPERS
three pairs

RIDING BOOTS
two pairs

*Cloaks, muffs, stoles, gloves,
and other essential
accessories, as required*

Hi! This is Princess Emily saying hello. I'm so happy you're here with us at Silver Towers. Charlotte, Katie, Daisy, Alice, Sophia, and I have such a good time, except when horrid Princess Diamonde and her twin sister, Gruella, try to spoil everything, of course.

We'd been keeping our fingers crossed, hoping that we'd gotten enough tiara points to get our Silver Sashes, but suddenly it was nearly time for the Silver Ball. And we began to panic—especially me!

Chapter One

*D*oes being nervous ever make you do silly things? The Silver Ball was only a week away and I was trying to keep calm, but it was so difficult. Honestly, every time I looked at a clock I could see the minutes disappearing! I couldn't stop thinking, *Will I have enough tiara points?* And that meant I kept getting things wrong.

On Monday, we had a lesson in Cutting Ribbons. Prince Dandino was in charge, and he told us to imagine we were cutting the ribbon to open a new library.

"Now," he said, "everybody will be watching, so you must be Perfect Princesses." He marched across to the workroom cabinet and came back with a large pair of scissors and a length of colored ribbon. "Princess Diamonde and Princess Charlotte, please take one end each and hold it tight. And we'll ask

Princess Emily to be our first guest princess. Make your speech, Princess Emily, then cut the ribbon."

We'd each made up a speech for homework, but as I stood up, my mind went blank.

"Um . . . ," I began. "That is . . .
I mean, I'm very happy . . . uh . . ."

Prince Dandino frowned.
"Emily," he said, "if you haven't
learned your speech by heart, please
read it."

"Yes, Your Highness," I said, but

as I picked up my bag, I remem-
bered where my homework was.
On my bedside table! I felt so
stupid.

"I'm very sorry, Your Highness,"
I mumbled. "It's in the Silver Rose
Room."

Prince Dandino sighed. "Never mind. Let's see what Princess Diamonde can do."

Diamonde looked so smug. She gave a perfect speech with no *uh*s or *um*s at all. As she finished, she tried to cut the ribbon, but the scissors were too blunt. At once, she whipped a tiny penknife out of her pocket and cut the ribbon neatly in two. "There!" she said,

and she turned to me. "That's how to open a library! I've watched Mommy do it a hundred times."

Of course, Diamonde got tons of tiara points. We could tell because Prince Dandino took out his notebook. While he wrote, he kept saying how smart she was to bring her penknife. She really was smart. Almost everyone else really struggled to cut the ribbon with the blunt scissors. Princess Gruella tugged so hard she nearly pulled Princess Sophia over. Only Princess Freya managed to cut it properly, and Prince Dandino nodded and scribbled down more points.

"Well done," he said. "Those scissors are very blunt. But Perfect Princesses must be prepared for all kinds of difficulties. Emily, I'm afraid I must give you two minus points unless you can show me your speech by the end of the day. Class dismissed!"

As we trailed away down the corridor, my friends tried to cheer me up. "You'll be okay," Katie said. "Just bring him your speech at lunch!"

"We all know you knew it really well." Alice patted my arm.

I began to feel a little bit better, but when I brought Prince Dandino my homework he gave me a sad shake of the head.

"It isn't like you to be so forgetful,

Princess Emily," he told me. "I hope you don't think that because it's nearly the end of the year you don't have to try."

That made me feel awful. What if I had almost earned enough tiara points to get my Silver Sash, but not quite? Was Prince Dandino trying to tell me something?

Chapter Two

On Tuesday, things weren't much better. Our principal, Queen Samantha Joy, said being a Perfect Princess is hard work, and we need to stay in shape. In addition to PE (Princess Exercises), we have game days. Usually they're really fun, but

I was still worrying about tiara points and I forgot my shoes. It was the first time I'd forgotten them, and our school Fairy Godmother (she's named Fairy Angora) was very nice about it, but I had to sit on the side and watch. It was so boring! What made it worse was

that Diamonde doesn't play games, and I had to sit with her. She spent the whole time telling me that games are for little kids, and making nasty remarks.

"Gruella's making such a fool of herself," she said. "Mommy told us we were never to behave like

hooligans, but just look at her! And look at Sophia! Her hair's so messy!"

I didn't answer, but Diamonde went on and on until at last I got angry. I know I should have just ignored her, but I couldn't. She was being so nasty!

I said, "And I suppose you think you're absolutely perfect! Well, I think you're stuck up and mean!" And at exactly that moment, Fairy Angora came to see if we were all right, and she heard me.

"Oh, Princess Emily!" she said. She looked so sad.

"It's quite all right, Fairy Angora,"

Diamonde said, and she sighed in a totally made-up way. "I forgive Princess Emily. I know she's

jealous, and I forgive her."

Honestly, I could have screamed. Is that very awful of me? I'm sure Perfect Princesses never ever think like that, but I did. I had to take a huge gulp of air before I could say, "Thank you, Diamonde. And I'm very sorry for what I said."

Fairy Angora floated off to help Sophia hold the winning tape, and she didn't say anything else to me the rest of the day. It made me feel even worse, because I just knew I'd disappointed her.

That night, I had a dream that I was trying to find my friends but they had disappeared. In my dream, I knew they'd gone to the Silver Ball without me because I didn't have enough tiara points, and I kept hearing Fairy Angora saying, "Oh, Princess Emily!" in such a sad way.

On Wednesday, our first class was Etiquette and Deportment. Queen Mother Matilda showed us how to welcome important visitors with a Sweeping Curtsey and Fluttering Fan. When it was my turn to curtsey, I could see Queen Mum Mattie looking at me, and I couldn't help remembering all the things that had gone wrong already that week. Something inside me knew she was expecting me to make a mistake, and I did. I wobbled, waved my arms, and fell flat on the floor! I felt terrible.

What was weird was that my

friends didn't do much better. Alice got confused and curtsied at the same time as Sophia, and they bumped heads. And then it turned out that Charlotte and Princess Katie had both forgotten their fans.

So we all ended up with only one tiara point each. Diamonde was the only one in the whole class who got five. She was so pleased with herself, she went around for the rest of the morning with her nose in the air.

At lunchtime that day, none of us from the Silver Rose Room was very chatty. Even Princess Alice didn't have much to say.

"Are you okay?" Sophia asked.

Alice put down her knife and fork and leaned across the table.

"I couldn't sleep last night," she

whispered. "I kept having a nightmare that everyone went to the Silver Ball except me. Isn't that silly?"

I stared at her. "But that's what I was dreaming!"

"Me, too," Sophia said, and Princess Daisy and Charlotte nodded.

"I've been having that dream for *weeks*," Katie said, and grinned. "I wish you'd told me. I thought it was only me!"

Chapter Three

*I*sn't it strange? When you find out someone else is as worried as you, somehow it makes you feel better.

"What exactly happens if we don't have enough tiara points?" I asked.

Alice shook her head. "I don't

know. When my big sister was at Silver Towers, everyone earned their Silver Sashes."

"I wish we knew how we were doing." Charlotte sighed. "Fairy Angora always tells us when she gives us points, but Prince Dandino just writes them in his little note-book."

"I'm sure Queen Samantha Joy doesn't always tell us everything either," Katie said. "She was watching us in assembly this morning, and when Diamonde wouldn't let Freya share her songbook, I'm absolutely sure she wrote something down."

Just as Katie finished speaking, who should come into the dining hall but our principal. And Fairy Angora was with her.

"My dear princesses," Queen Samantha Joy began, "Prince Dandino and Queen Mother Matilda have told me that many of

you are finding it hard to concentrate on your lessons, and your
work is suffering as a consequence."

Honestly, I nearly fell off my
chair. I could feel myself turning
red, and the most terrible thought
came into my head.

Queen Samantha Joy was going to tell us we weren't invited to the Silver Ball!

"It is my suspicion that some of you are getting overly anxious about your Silver Sashes," our principal went on. "I would like to take this opportunity to promise that if you have worked hard and done your best, you have no need to worry at all. Now, I have spoken with Fairy Angora, and we have come up with a plan to help you enjoy your last days at Silver Towers. Fairy Angora, would you like to explain?" And Queen Samantha Joy sat down, her eyes twinkling.

Fairy Angora was looking so excited. "My little darlings," she said. "We are going to have such fun! You are going to help with the preparations for the Silver Banquet and the Silver Ball! Lady Victoria Allpepper is, at this very moment, waiting in the lower hall to help you plan a banquet fit for emperors. Tomorrow, we will organize the decorations and make Silver Towers look utterly beautiful. On Friday, we'll tidy up, and on Saturday we'll have a late breakfast because you'll be up very late that night. I can't tell you why, because it's a secret, but"—Fairy Angora stopped and beamed—"it has to do with wishes and a star!"

At once, everyone began to clap wildly, except for Diamonde. She

was sitting behind me, and I heard her say, "Really, Gruella! Mommy doesn't pay for us to put up decorations! I certainly won't do anything so pathetic! Just because *some* people can't even curtsey doesn't mean we should be treated like servants!"

I knew she wanted me to hear her, but I didn't turn around. I waited for Gruella to say something mean as well, but she didn't. She said, "Actually, I think it sounds really fun." Then she squeezed herself onto the bench in between Daisy and me.

"You didn't mean to fall over when you curtsied, did you, Emily?" she asked.

I was so astonished! Daisy's eyes were wide, and Alice, Charlotte, Katie, and Sophia were trying their best not to stare.

"Can I be your partner when we're planning the banquet?" Gruella asked me. "Please say yes! I'm really good at things like banquets. Mommy's are just the best!"

Chapter Four

I felt so weird. For a moment I couldn't say anything at all. Ever since I've been at the Academy, I've had the same very best friends, and we've always done everything together. Diamonde and Gruella don't usually want anything to do with us; they think they're too special, especially Diamonde. But at that moment, one of the Princess Rules floated into my head: *Perfect Princesses never have favorites. They are equally kind to all they meet.*

"All right, Gruella," I said. I didn't sound very enthusiastic, so I quickly added, "That'll be fun. I'd sort of promised Daisy and the others, but please come and join us. We can all work together."

Behind me Diamonde said, "Oh. I see. Little Princess Emily is trying to get back at me by leaving me out. See if I care!" And she flounced off on her own.

That afternoon, we had such a good time, even though Gruella was really bossy. We were allowed to choose all our favorite foods, and we designed the most amazing celebration cake. Of course, the top was crowned with seven Silver Towers.

"Please tell me, what did Fairy Angora mean about wishes and a star?" Gruella asked Lady Victoria as we were cleaning up at the end of the lesson.

Lady Victoria raised her eyebrows. "That," she said, "is a secret, as I'm sure Fairy Angora made clear."

"But is it something nice?" Gruella wanted to know.

"You'll find out on Saturday night," Lady Victoria said firmly.

By the time Saturday actually arrived, I'd almost forgotten about the surprise. Thursday and Friday had whizzed by, and none of us had had any more bad dreams. It was only on Saturday morning that we woke up with butterflies in our stomachs. When we sat down for breakfast, Gruella was the only one who could eat anything. She was still insisting on doing everything with us, and I was almost getting used to her. If only I hadn't had an annoying little feeling in the back of my mind. Why was she being so friendly?

When we got up from the table, I saw Diamonde sitting all by herself at the other end of the room.

"Is she okay?" I asked Gruella.

"Oh, yes," she said loudly. "Diamonde's fine." And she put her arm through mine.

"Doesn't she mind you leaving her all alone?" I asked. "Isn't she lonely?"

Gruella sniffed. "Serves her right. She always thinks she's the best at everything!" She looked over her shoulder at Diamonde and sneered. "Well, she isn't best at making friends." And Gruella tried to march me out of the dining hall.

"Just a minute," I said, and I slipped back to Diamonde.

"Diamonde," I began, "I know we haven't always gotten along very well, but if you want to sit with us at the banquet, we'd be very happy to have you."

"No thanks," Diamonde said without looking up.

"Well, if you change your mind, you can," I said, and I left her sitting there.

Chapter Five

*A*s we got changed into our beautiful dresses for the Silver Banquet that evening, I kept thinking about Diamonde. Even as Charlotte helped me do up my dress—it was a really pretty sea-green silk with a zigzagging hem—I couldn't really concentrate.

"What are you daydreaming about?" Charlotte asked me.

"I was thinking how lucky I am to have friends," I said slowly. "And how Diamonde doesn't even have Gruella anymore."

Charlotte gave me a hug. "You'd be sorry for a lonely slug, Emily," she told me. "Come on, put your shoes on!"

Even though we'd helped to decorate the dining hall, we couldn't help gasping as we walked in for the Silver Banquet. The walls were hung with glittering silver ribbons, and there were rows of candles shining on every table. The celebration cake looked amazing, and a tiny bright star was circling around and around the tallest tower! It was magical.

We almost forgot to be nervous as we ate the delicious cakes and cream and peaches and pies, and it was only as we left the dining hall to go to the Silver Ballroom that the butterflies began to flutter in our stomachs again.

"Will they call us in by name?" Alice whispered as we walked slowly and steadily two by two down the long marble corridor.

"I don't know," I whispered back. "Oh, Alice! What if—"

"Shh!" she said. "Remember

what Queen Samantha Joy said!"

Then we were at the doors of the ballroom and Queen Samantha Joy was waiting in the doorway. As we walked in, she handed us each a Silver Sash and we curtsied. I was so surprised, I could hardly manage

to whisper a thank-you.

Once we all had our sashes, we were asked to stand quietly while Queen Samantha Joy swept up to the stage.

"Good evening, my very dear princesses," she said. "Welcome, and please listen carefully. At midnight, we will climb the stairs to the top of Silver Towers and we will hold hands as we wait for the Wishing Star. If it comes, and I really hope that it will, then—and only then—you will truly be able to say that you have earned your Silver Sashes!"

At once there was a babble of voices. Queen Samantha Joy held up her hand for silence. "While we wait, let's enjoy ourselves. Please take your partners for the first dance of the Silver Ball!"

The musicians burst into a wonderfully happy tune. Gruella

grabbed Daisy and whizzed her onto the dance floor. Alice and Charlotte and I danced together, and Sophia and Katie twirled past us at a dizzying speed.

It was fabulous! We danced and

we danced, and we were almost breathless by the time the music stopped and Queen Samantha Joy announced that the time had come to go to the top of Silver Towers.

As we climbed up and up the spiral staircase, we were silent. There was something very important and serious in the way Queen Samantha Joy strode in front of us, and we felt the same when we finally reached the rooftop. Somehow it felt as if there was going to be a very special and serious ceremony.

A huge moon was turning the world around us silver, and it was so quiet! Prince Dandino and Fairy

Angora shushed us with their fingers on their lips, and we tiptoed into a circle.

"Princesses of Silver Towers," Queen Samantha Joy said in a

hushed whisper. "Please take one another's hands. Make sure that nobody is left out or the Wishing Star will not come to us."

It was almost scary. We were

wide-eyed as we held hands, and I was really pleased when Charlotte gave my fingers a squeeze. Gruella was on my other side, in between Alice and me, and even *she* was looking anxious.

"Are we ready?" Queen Samantha Joy asked.

Everyone nodded, and then I saw Diamonde. She was standing all by herself in the dark shadows. Her arms were firmly folded and she was staring at Gruella with such a mean look. She was angry and lonely.

Fairy Angora had already begun to count in her soft, sweet voice.

"Ten," she said. "Nine. Eight—"

I made up my mind. "Quick!" I whispered to Gruella, and I half pulled and half dragged her as I slipped behind the circle and ran to Diamonde.

"Seven. Six."

Across the circle, I saw Charlotte and Alice close the gap we'd left.

"Five. Four."

"Gruella! *Take her hand!*" I knew I was hissing, but I had to make Gruella understand.

"Three. Two."

"Please!" I said, and I pushed us into the circle. I held Gruella's hand tightly and snatched Princess Lisa's hand, and as Gruella took Diamonde's hand, Fairy Angora said, "One!"

For a moment there was nothing. Nothing, except the silvery moonlight.

Chapter Six

The whole sky lit up as the
Wishing Star zoomed down.
Around and around the top of the
tower it flew, around and around—
until it exploded into a million tiny
stars. They were everywhere I
looked. They twinkled in the air,

and in our hair, and on our dresses, but most of all they sparkled and shone on our Silver Sashes.

There was a loud fanfare of

trumpets, and our teachers clapped and cheered.

"Well done, princesses!" Queen Samantha Joy boomed. "Well done

indeed! Wear your sashes and be proud! And one last thing—don't forget to make a wish before you leave the tower."

A wish! As I hurried toward my

friends, an idea popped into my head. Before I had time to change my mind, I said out loud, "I wish Diamonde was as happy as me!"

"Well wished, Princess Emily."

Queen Samantha Joy was beside me, with Fairy Angora. "Well wished indeed. And, as our star pupil, would you like to lead us down the stairs and back to the Silver Ballroom?"

"Star pupil?" I gasped.

"Of course," Fairy Angora said. "Just look at your sash!"

I looked down and I could hardly believe what I saw. My sash was *covered* in stars!

"Dear Princess Emily," Fairy Angora said with such a sweet smile, "you have the heart of a Perfect Princess. It's easy to be friends with those we love, but to make friends with an enemy is truly admirable."

As I looked at Alice and Charlotte and Sophia and Katie and Daisy, I could see they had

starry sashes too. Only Diamonde had no stars at all, but she didn't seem to mind. She was laughing and laughing at something Gruella had said, and she really did look happy.

That night, as we sank into our beds in our wonderful Silver Rose Room, our sashes sparkled in the dark.

"Wow," Charlotte said sleepily. "What an evening!"

"Yes," Alice agreed. "But it would have gone so wrong if it hadn't been for Emily!"

"Three cheers for Emily," Daisy

said. "Hip hip—"

"Wait a minute," I interrupted. "If we're going to have three cheers, I know what it's got to be for. It's

got to be three cheers for friends, for the best friends ever."

So that's what we cheered for!

And did we cheer for you too? Of course we did!

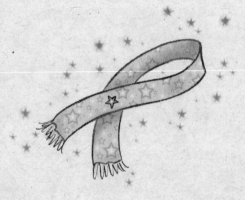

Join us at Ruby Mansions!
Find out what happens in . . .

Princess Chloe
~ AND THE ~
Primrose Petticoats

Oh, I'm so excited! I mean, here we are at Ruby Mansions, learning to be Perfect Princesses. Isn't that just so amazing? And you're here too. Hurray! I'm so glad you can keep us company.

I'm Princess Chloe. Have I told you that? You might have met the Rose Room Princesses already—Charlotte, Katie, Daisy, Alice, Sophia, and Emily. I'm in the Poppy Room, and so are Jessica, Georgia, Olivia, Lauren, and Amy. And we're all special friends. We're going to have so much fun!

You are cordially invited
to the Royal Princess Academy

**Follow the adventures of your special princess friends
as they try to earn enough points to join the Tiara Club.**

Katherine Tegen Books
An Imprint of HarperCollinsPublishers